The Phantom Sock Snatcher

by A.J.Stairmand

Illustrations by Louisa Kewell

ISBN: 978-0-9569234-9-3
A CIP catalogue record for this book is available
from the British Library.

Book Design: Jon Gay, Seesaw Design
www.seesaw-design.co.uk

Published by: Stairmand Publishing 2014

Printed by: Wyndeham Grange Ltd
Butts Road, Southwick, West Sussex, BN42 4EJ

Distributed by: York Publishing Services
64 Hallfield Road, Layerthorpe, York YO31 7ZQ

About the author

Anne (Stairmand) has worked with London boroughs and was the author in residence for Barking and Dagenham Libraries in September 2013. She has given children's workshops at literary festivals for Waltham Forest, Barking and Dagenham and has also linked with libraries in other counties. She is currently involved in the 'Pen to Print' project with Barking and Dagenham working with primary schools in the borough. She has also led writer's workshops for aspiring adult writers.

Acknowledgements

I would like to thank Sharon Cairns, Sharon Burns, the editing company The Book Specialist, and Jon Gay at Seesaw Design for his contributions in helping and preparing the book. I would also like to thank Louisa for such amusing and clever illustrations which make the characters come alive. Finally, I would like to thank my family Michael, James and Will, my father and friends for their humour, laughter and amazing support.

Chapter 1

The Wumple Chumple planted another row of socks, making sure the colours and patterns didn't clash. Delving into an enormous sack which overflowed with socks of every shape, size, colour, pattern and texture, he put them into pairs so they all matched. Slowly scratching his head, he couldn't quite believe there were so many shades of purple.

Gazing at the huge sock trees, the Wumple Chumple smiled. He loved his sock trees, his sock plants, and his sock hedges. Looking around, he saw pink-spotted birds flying above the blue trees. Green lambs and blue horses played in the fields and the pale blue grass wafted in the soft summer breeze.

The Wumple Chumple thought how perfect his life was. He loved flying through the air at night in his magic cart with his three friends, the Idgits, to another world where he would gather socks from children's bedrooms before bringing them back to his land to plant and grow.

He had been collecting socks for a

long time and had visited many places and houses. His magic ponies would wait outside each house, cantering in the air, whilst the Idgits and the Wumple Chumple dropped into bedrooms through the window or wall. And whilst the children slept, they gathered the socks, and then disappeared the same way, through the wall or windows. As he thought about the coming adventure that night, the Wumple Chumple sat by a river watching as it whooshed and splooshed against stones and small rocks.

'This is just wonderful,' he sighed.

The Wumple Chumple gathered up stray socks. Staring at them, he said, 'Now why don't you fit in my row?' The socks couldn't answer – but they did appear left out. 'Perhaps I could plant you indoors.'

He gathered the remainder of them, placed them in his sack and put the trowel

into the pocket of his woven sock coat. Feeling tired after his morning's gardening, he decided to go home and have a bite to eat. Home was an old cottage, built from tinted bricks and stone, at the top of a blue and orange hill. It was dishevelled and crumbling in places. The gaps in the crumbling walls were filled and patched up with an assortment of socks to make them look bright and cheerful from a distance.

The red and green tiles, placed on the roof in a haphazard, dazzlingly, deliciously fun sort of way, also added to the brightness of his house. The broken chimney was wrapped in hundreds of tied socks, to stop it falling down. As he gazed at his wonderful cottage the Wumple

Chumple sighed. Style was definitely his strong point.

After eating some of his magic soup and something that looked like a huge ice cream, he went into a dim, empty room. Velvety darkness smothered everything, except for the hazy light from a large glass globe which gently pulsed on a table in the centre of the room. He walked towards to it and nervously pulled a pair of glasses out of his pocket. He put them on and peered into the globe, looking intently.

'Oh, oh, oh! No, this can't be happening. Oh no!' he muttered loudly, unhappy at something. He turned away from the globe, he took the glasses off and wiped his crestfallen eyes. He was crying. Something

had upset the Wumple Chumple.

Hiding in the room, three pairs of beady eyes peered at the lonely figure. The Wumple Chumple turned towards a tall black bookcase bulging with huge, thick, dusty books. He scoured the shelves and, smiling, carefully picked a book. It wasn't just any book, as it gurgled and flapped its pages open and shut, billowing gusts of dust into the air. Then, howling, it stood upright in the Wumple Chumple's hands and spoke.

'I was having a long sleep. It's not time to wake up yet. I'm tired. Put me back to sleep. An old spell book like me needs its sleep. And, my dear Wumple Chumple, I am not getting involved in any mad magic ideas. I am old and I'm tired!'

The book promptly snapped shut and started snoring. It was not going to do anything requested. The Wumple Chumple smiled. He was sure the spell book would help him, just like it had done so many times before. Patting the book, he put it on the table by the pulsing globe. Once again he was dazzled by the images of the tragedy pictured in it. And so he sobbed again, whilst the spell book snored and puffed as it slept.

'Dear friend, we have spells to cast in a faraway place. I fear I will need all the help I can muster. My dear spell book, I am going to need you to save these children in the globe,' he muttered gently to the book in a caring way. '**But I'm not ready to wake up yet, Wumple!** Can't you wait just a couple more hundred years? I am an old spell book now, not as fast, not as good, and I forget potions and spells!' pleaded the battered and torn spell book.

The Wumple Chumple shook his head and replied, 'I'm afraid not. We have spells to perform, and we have some magic work to do. I must say, it's been a long time since I had to use it in a different world. I'm not sure if I can use my spells too. '

Chapter 2

The Wumple Chumple's conversation with the spell book had been watched by his three little friends who often stayed in his cottage to help him and keep him company. The Idgits were small in height, only reaching his knee, and had known the Wumple Chumple for hundreds of years. They talked very fast in squeaky voices and were quite bossy, but were very kind and good-hearted. They were hiding behind a great old chest and staring intently with folded arms.

One of them whispered sharply to the others, 'I wish the Wumple Chumple wouldn't look at things which upset him. I mean, look at what goes on down there in this other world. Look what happens to him! And I don't know what that old spell book's going to do – the Wumple Chumple hasn't used it for hundreds of years. Everyone knows the spell book's old and moody!'

A tiny creature raised and pointed a long nail on the end of a knobbly finger to the others behind the chest, who agreed. Dark, glinting eyes focused on the large figure of the Wumple Chumple bending over the globe, so unhappy.

One of the other Idgits added, 'I don't think he should use the globe any more. Look how he acts when he watches it.'

'If only he hadn't found the globe...' added yet another, rather high-pitched voice from behind the chest.

The Wumple Chumple had found the globe under a huge mound of blue soil in the woods on a walk one day and had brought it home. He didn't know what it was used for, so in the beginning the object was a source of bewilderment. At first, he had used it as a lamp in the cottage because it glowed. His friends, the Idgits, decided that was boring, so they had plotted to sneak it out and play with it. After struggling to find a way up to the table, they decided to use some small ladders and lean them against it. Once they finally got the globe, they took it outside and played with it in the garden. They liked rolling it around like a giant football. Nobody had known it was magic at that time.

The globe's real role was discovered when the Wumple Chumple was cleaning and polishing it one day after the Idgits had played with it in the garden. Suddenly, it started to display images of people from a different world. It revealed a different place where people weren't always safe and sometimes suffered.

Once he became familiar with its

changing pictures and images, the Wumple Chumple realised the globe was telling him about events which were happening in an unknown land. And now he was seeing terrible suffering in a place which

may need his help and his magic.

Unaware of the Idgits secretly watching him, the Wumple Chumple stared into the globe. He saw an image of a little boy and girl crying, surrounded by smoke and fire and other people wailing. He couldn't make out any clear images except of the children who clung to each other screaming and shouting out names.

They appeared lost and the place looked so frightening. Mountains of rubble which once had been buildings covered the land like a sea, the sand and cement creating smog and smoke. Squashed and broken vehicles lay flattened and crushed like tissue paper, flattened under the weight of the buildings. Broken glass and flames from small and large fires swarmed the area like vampires sucking any life left.

Amidst all this were people wandering weakly, dragging themselves to safety and searching for families and loved ones. And the sky loomed overhead like an angry monster, dark, dangerous and cold, uncaring and cruel.

This was not like the Wumple Chumple's cluttered world of socks that had so many wonderful uses, looked so good and was safe.

He had been following the plight of the children each day; their sorrow made him cry. The globe had given him a sign: it was sending him a message, a signal that he had to help them.

He wanted to help them.
He wanted to save them.

He wanted to bring them to his beautifully coloured and gaily decorated cottage where they could run and play forever and ever.

Chapter 3

Cautiously, the Idgits sneaked out from behind the well-placed chest, tiptoed up to their crying friend giving him a cloth to blow his nose. Each one looked thoughtfully at the Wumple Chumple bent over the globe and each one muttered sternly at him. They didn't like to see him so upset and sad.

'Here you are, have this,' said Bendrick,
scratching his small green ears and blowing
his blue hair out of his eyes. Dressed in
a yellow tunic and short, black, pointed
boots on tiny feet, he placed his chubby
hands, with wide, curling nails, on his
stout, round hips. The Idgit peered into
the Wumple Chumple's face and frowned

at him.

'Oh, don't do that, Bendrick! Look at them! Look into the magic globe at these children and see what's happening! We must do something… And the spell book will help – I just know it. I hope it can cast one of its spells to help these children,' said the Wumple Chumple, only to be interrupted by another Idgit, Beezo – a smaller, much thinner version of Bendrick, but dressed exactly the same.

'We can't save them. Their place is different. They don't have blue grass. We have to be sensible about this, Wumple. The globe will have to go… And also that old, forgetful and bad-tempered spell book. We don't want it around. It puts any old rubbish together and hopes it works,' said Beezo, firmly folding his arms and glaring at everyone, just to show his disapproval.

'We could save them and bring them here when we go down to get the socks tonight. They could live here until they were older an' stronger!' butted in Breanok, a thinner and even smaller Idgit who had noticed the hurt and sadness in his big friend's eyes.

The other two Idgits turned their heads sharply and, curling their mouths and squinting, glared at Breanok. He was meant to agree with everything they said!

Breanok pointed to the other two Idgits and stamped his feet to get their attention.

Finally, Bendrick said, 'Wumple, you get too upset when you see what's happening in the globe. Let's put it away for you, and then you can just get on planting an' looking after all your growing socks. That's a much better idea!'

Bendrick tried not to stare at the faces of the children in the globe, who were still clinging to each other and crying for their parents. Then he peered more closely.

Behind the children there was smoke, shattered buildings and a blackness which seemed to show that something terrible had happened.

Taken aback by the scene, Bendrick said thoughtfully, 'On second thoughts, Wumple, perhaps we should take a look there tonight after we've got more socks. We could fly the cart to that part of the world and see if we could help the children. Maybe we should take the magic blankets, to keep them warm and safe if we see them…

'And I suppose we'll have to take 'it', won't we? I hope it doesn't make that disgusting noise when we're flying. And I'm not sitting next to it!' snapped Bendrick, looking at the huge, tattered spell book which snored, spluttered and puffed as it slept.

'We could save the children, just like superheroes,' added Breanok, smiling and jumping at the thought of having a further adventure after collecting socks from houses.

The three Idgits stared up at the towering figure of the Wumple Chumple, and clapped their hands in glee.

The Wumple Chumple grabbed Breanok and gave him a huge hug. 'Yes, we could save them and bring them back here to live happily ever after,' he gabbled. Then he stopped. 'But what do they eat and drink? Will they live here happily?'

The three Idgits looked puzzled. They couldn't see eating and drinking their magic food and water as a problem – everybody loved their magic food. Besides, the spell book would sort something out. They chattered amongst themselves, delighted at their new plan to find and save the children. However, secretly they were a little frightened at the thought of their new adventure – where it would take them and what they would find.

Chapter 4

The Idgits talked about the flight in the magic cart, knowing they were collecting more socks for planting. 'So which houses are we going to get our socks from when we fly tonight?' asked Beezo. He glanced around the room and at the list of places scribbled and drawn on the wall where the Wumple Chumple kept all his magic travelling plans and routes to different stars and galaxies and worlds.

The Wumple Chumple answered, 'Before we save the children we're going back to that young Joe's house. You remember him, don't you? He does all that running around on a field with a ball, and gets dirty and messy with lots of other boys. Anyway, he has bags of socks, all different colours. His mother's got him loads of socks. Loads of them. His mum just keeps buying more. They're good quality and wonderful colours, which will make my trees look amazing, don't you think?' The Idgits shook their heads and Breanok added, 'Oh, and so have his friends. Anyway, Wumple, how are your sock trees growing this year? Have you any amazing mixes?'

But the Wumple Chumple reminded his friends of their important mission to save the children, and told them to prepare the ponies. Then he placed a dark cloth over the globe and hurried to get ready for tonight. Although he loved to admire his sock garden, today he was thinking about the children in the globe.

On his way to see the ponies, the Wumple Chumple glanced at the garden and thought just how wonderfully his newly planted socks were growing. The colours were blooming in the sunlight, enjoying the heat, and they made such a fine display. Each one was unique, a bit like flowers – different species but together they blended to make a perfect picture. He was so proud of his sock garden, and all his friends praised its brightness and wealth of colour.

His thoughts returned to the children. He was sure with the globe, his magic blankets, his blue ponies and the golden rays from his cart he would find the children. He would rescue them.

Chapter 5

Each night the Wumple Chumple and the Idgits clambered into a spindly magic cart which had sparkling wheels that shone in the moonlight. It flew through the midnight sky and changed colour with the breeze. They checked the cart was safe, checked they had bags for the socks and checked the ponies had been fed. The healthy ponies, with their glistening manes, lean, strong limbs, and loud, neighing noises loved soaring through the sky,, skimming the stars and galaxies with the Wumple Chumple and the Idgits.

Preparing for the evening flight with the Wumple Chumple always excited the Idgits. They loved flying with the ponies pulling the magic cart and enjoyed looking at the beautiful stars which shone like diamonds.

'I love it when their manes sort of float and waft in the air,' whispered Breanok to Beezo as he stroked the ponies.

Nuzzling up to Breanok, the three ponies smiled, fluttered their long eyelashes at him and opened their mouths for treats. Breanok patted each one on the nose gently and shovelled his other knobbly hand into a glistening sack digging out handfuls of tiny, shimmering grains and splaying them out in readiness. Each handful was devoured by the excited ponies – they kicked their hind legs into the air, thrilled to have their favourite food given by Breanok, who was the softest and kindest of the Idgits. He laughed at them, whispered words into their ears, rustled their manes, stroked the crowns of their heads and patted their backs when the grains disappeared. All gave satisfied grunts.

'Breanok, what are you doing now?' shouted an impatient Bendrick, rushing to the cart. He was carrying the magic sacks, which he folded into the cart. 'We're going soon, so you'd better get the ponies ready to be reined up for the flight. Oh, and don't forget to bring some grain this time, so they don't get hungry,' he added, fastening the sacks carefully inside the cart.

After feeding the ponies, Beezo had gone to help the Wumple Chumple. Now he carried the magic globe to the cart, to use later when they would search for the children. Always the organised and bossy one, he was generally left to get things ready for magic journeys.

'We need to make sure they're ready to go soon,' reminded Bendrick, scrambling into the cart along with Beezo and ensuring they were fastened in tight.

The Wumple Chumple followed his little friend, putting two magic blankets and his spell book, which was still a little grumpy, into the cart. Placing the grumbling spell book next to him, he checked everything. He looked into the sky, ready to navigate the cart, and felt the whirl of the breeze whistling around him.

'Where are you off to now?' the breeze asked, blowing the summer air between the shafts of wood. The soft, warm air slithered down to caress the wheels, which were gleaming and glistening.

'We're going back for more socks. Then we're off to save a little boy and girl who have lost their parents,' chirped Breanok, smiling at the thought of the children joining in his world, settling into a life of amusement, games – and planting socks. It seemed so exciting and wonderful to help the children, and he was so sure they could.

After checking they had everything, the Wumple Chumple and his three comrades were ready to fly off for their adventure.

Once they had all clambered into the cart, it shuffled and swayed from side to side and the golden wheels started to spin. The ponies shook their manes and tails, tapped the ground with their hooves and reared as they prepared to fly. The Idgits grabbed their seats and the Wumple Chumple clutched his hat as the cart and gathering even more speed, shot into the sky like a rocket flying into space. As the cart climbed in the sky it became faster and more powerful.

The Wumple Chumple laughed and waved at the passing stars, which glowed serenely as if to welcome the travelling guests through the galaxies. Every now and then they touched the rays of a bustling star, always in a hurry to brighten up a new part of the endless skies, leaving a fine mist in its wake. The golden path disappeared into the far distance until there was only a pinprick of sparkle making a faint glitter trail across the sky.

'I wonder what we'd find out there,' pondered Bendrick, following the slithers with his eyes and trying to imagine the new, undiscovered worlds which they hadn't visited yet.

'I don't know why you're bothering

about that,' retorted Beezo. 'We have enough trouble getting more socks.'

From his perch on the seat of the cart, the Wumple Chumple laughed. Steering gently with the reins, he spoke to his ponies, encouraging them not to get tired and soothing their anxieties about the journey. Enjoying the magic ride, the group of friends smiled and waved at the passing stars.

Breanok commented that it was always good to go back to a place they liked. The group nodded. They liked Joe's house, his bedroom, and

lovvvvvvvved

his socks!

Having emptied Joe's sock drawer quite

a few times, the travellers were familiar with how to get to his house. However, they had a feeling that their sock borrowing might be causing Joe some trouble with his mother. She was annoyed with her son. All the new socks she bought just seemed to disappear. And worse, Joe didn't even have a decent excuse…

Chapter 6

It wasn't quite so perfect where Joe Ridgewell lived with his mother and father, in a village in a different world from that of the Wumple Chumple and the Idgits.

'I can't find any socks – again!' growled Joe as he crawled under his bed to check if there were any spare ones hiding under a mound of rubbish. He really was getting tired of this problem, which had been

happening for the last couple of weeks.

Shouting downstairs to his mother, he asked her where his socks were. A sharp voice boomed up to his bedroom letting Joe know that his mother was not in a good mood. This was a worry, because his mother had a terrible temper when roused.

'I put all your clothes out last night

with a clean pair of socks!' she yelled up the stairs. 'You'd better be quick – you'll be late for school and you haven't had your breakfast!' His mother slammed the kitchen door as she finished her sentence.

Joe sat on his bed and wondered where

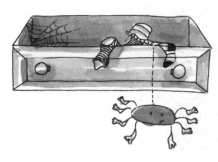

his socks were. He was sure he had seen them when he brushed his teeth. Annoyed, he scoured the bedroom once more and found two odd socks, both grey, both too small, one stuffed in a drawer and the other in a games bag. He squeezed his feet into them. He looked more than daft and his football team would laugh at him.

Making sure his trousers covered the socks and only his shoes peeked out, Joe slung the duvet over the bed, chucked his books under it and combed his hair. He grabbed his books and school bag, and bounded down the stairs.

His father was sitting, having his

breakfast and reading the morning paper.

He was commenting on the main stories and some news articles to Joe's mother. Joe sat down, he was not listening.

In the background the main points from the news on television blurred with the chatter and music from the radio, and the continual clatter of his mother emptying the dishwasher made it difficult to understand anything at all.

Looking up, Joe's father munched on his toast and asked,

'**So,** what's happening today, Joe?'

'Nothing much Dad. Got to get the team sorted out and let the new PE teacher know the names of the boys playing this week. Also, I have training tonight. And Jack's asked if I want to have tea at his house sometime this week. So, not that much this week,' answered Joe, scoffing his toast and gulping his tea.

Suddenly, he looked down below the table. His father's feet had caught his eye.

On each foot was a different coloured sock, one the usual navy, the other black with orange stripes. Unable to control his laughter, Joe howled out, 'What's happened to your socks?'

Casually, as if it were perfectly normal, his dad replied, 'Oh, same problem as you. Except I'm not told off like you.' His father winked and smirked at Joe.

Joe chuckled and smiled. Nothing much fazed his dad, even wearing brightly coloured socks to work. 'And something else, Joe: because I'm a grownup, I can wear what I want. Nobody will say anything.'

Both of them laughed at the thought of his dad holding meetings with important people whilst wearing an orange-striped sock. With that, his father closed the paper and got ready to leave for work. It was even funnier when he kissed Joe's mother, who was too busy muttering about lazy boys to notice anything strange.

When his father had gone, Joe was left with the background sound of the television and radio to keep him company.

Chapter 7

At the door Joe's mother checked he had everything he needed for school. She brushed his blazer, re-tied his tie, inspected behind his ears (which he hated) and sniffed his breath to make sure he'd brushed his teeth (which he also hated). Then, handing him his scarf, she said, 'Have you got everything?' Pushing his lunch box into his bag, Joe's mother ushered him out of the front door with a wave and a big, sloppy kiss. Luckily, there was nobody from school waiting at the bus stop to laugh or make fun of him as he kissed his mother goodbye. He really didn't like this fuss in the morning. It didn't fit with his tough sportsman image.

Once on the bus, Joe started chatting with a friend. **'So, Larry, what's with the odd socks?'** asked Joe laughingly, pointing at Larry's jazzy socks – making sure he hid his own feet well under the bus seat. Leaning closer to Larry, he waited for an amusing answer. 'Dunno. My mum went mad this morning when I came downstairs with them on. I just couldn't find a pair anywhere and she shouted – boy did she shout! She says she's fed up of me losing one of my socks each day when she puts out a pair. Worse than that, she says I've got to use my pocket money to buy some now, just to show me where the money goes.'

Larry turned towards the window. Joe kept quiet. He'd had it easy in his house this morning.

How weird, he thought. All these socks and not a pair so far!

As the bus continued on its route, Joe took an interest in the socks of everyone getting on and finding a seat. Amazed at his observations, he noticed that nearly all those wearing socks had odd ones on. Maybe people were just too busy or too tired to notice what they were wearing first thing in the morning.

By the time the bus stopped at school it was raining and Joe wished he'd worn his big, thick coat. Huddling into his blazer, he rushed into the playground and found the nearest shelter, by the bikes. School wasn't open yet and everyone was trying to keep warm and dry. All the boys were squashed into the bike shelter, whilst the girls were standing quietly and orderly in the alcoves at the entrances to the classrooms.

Joe didn't mention the socks to anybody. He kept quiet until he heard Larry speaking. 'Yeah, well, my mum's so mad at me not having a pair of socks that I've got to buy some. How wicked is that?'

His fellow comrades nodded in agreement.

One of the other boys chirped up, 'Yeah, I just don't know where mine were this morning. I've had to nick one of my sister's and… it's a pale blue. I bet I get into trouble for this.' The boy looked down at his shoes and socks in disgust.

Joe had a lot of sympathy for him. Throughout his day at school, Joe did not listen to anything at all; he just concentrated on looking at every teacher to see whether his or her socks matched. Bemused, he found himself making a tally of teachers wearing odd socks and any wearing actual pairs. Most of the male teachers were wearing odd ones, but nobody seemed to think it was strange.

Assembly was given by the head teacher,
who always wore black socks to match his
black, shiny, tightly laced shoes. But today

it was different. Today Mr Grizzleton-Crimp was wearing a pink, frilly sock on his left foot and on his right, a yellow and red one which flashed when his foot moved. Joe stared, unable to stop sniggering as the head made the announcements for the coming week about sports fixtures.

At break, lunchtime and PE the conversations were not only about sports, the weekend and the matches to be played this coming week, but also about socks.

Some of the boys thought there was a burglar about; others thought they were just lost in the pipes of washing machines or dryers. Others were convinced there was a sock snatcher who crept into people's houses at night and stole their socks.

Later, back at home after school Joe put another pair of new socks which his mother had bought him in the top left-hand corner of his sock drawer, underneath a pile of vests. He decided that giving them to his mum would be a good idea. She could keep them in a safe place.

Downstairs in the kitchen, in between games on the computer, he gave the socks to his mother. Then he made a suggestion, partly to get into her good books and not to lose this new pair: 'Mum, I have an idea. You keep them and give them to me tomorrow. That way I won't get into trouble.'

'Alright. Put them back in my bedroom and I'll put them in one of the drawers by my dressing table. I'll give them to you in the morning.' Heaving a sigh of relief, Joe went back to his computer games. This decision had made him feel so much better. That night Joe went to sleep safe in the knowledge that his new socks were safe – or so he thought!

Chapter 8

It was the scream of anger and disbelief coming from his mother which woke Joe. She sounded wild and almost crazy.

Joe bolted upright in bed. He heard his father shouting at his mum to go back to sleep and not to wake people. Joe checked his watch and found that it wasn't time for him to get up. As he snuggled down into the duvet he wondered about his socks,

and then he slowly drifted back to sleep. Again, he was awoken by his mother shouting from her bedroom in a very, very angry voice.

'I just put them in a drawer near my dressing table and now they're gone! Where are they? I don't understand it!'

Joe's mum was furious about something. Joe turned to see the time on the alarm clock by the side of his bed, and then snuggled down beneath his duvet. His mum was always shouting about something in the morning. He didn't care. He just wanted a few more minutes sleep before getting up and getting ready for school. So he pulled his pillow over his head and burrowed down into the bed, and continued to slumber and snooze, happy in his land of dreams.

Charging into his bedroom, his mother demanded to know what Joe had done with his new socks. 'When did you take them? I thought you wanted me to look after them for you! Joe, are you listening?'

His mother stood at the bottom of his bed, tugging at the duvet wrapped tightly around him like a blanket. There was no reply, response or acknowledgment from beneath the mound of bedding. His mother shook the duvet, disturbing Joe's

haven of warmth and peace. A leg shook
as a sudden gust of cold air charged up the
bed, disturbing Joe's slumber.

'**Joe, are you listening to
me?** When did you take the socks?' his
mother demanded, obviously frustrated.
Joe sat bolt upright in his bed, his eyes
bleary, his head dizzy

and his body limp from his sleep. Startled,
he rubbed his eyes to see the looming
figure of a woman, his mother, bearing
down on him. Her hands were on her
hips, her mouth was pursed, ready for a

massive argument, and her shoulders were strong and wide. She looked as if she was ready to hit him.

He gave out a mild yell, taken aback by the rage of his mother.

'What are you talking about? I wanted you to have the socks so I wouldn't lose them. Anyway, you took them from me and put them in a drawer,' he blurted out, upset that his mother was accusing him of taking the socks.

'Joe, they're not in the drawer! You've taken them! What have you done with them?' demanded his mother. Indignantly, Joe scrambled out of bed and said he didn't have them. He didn't mind when he got in trouble for doing something wrong, but when he'd done nothing, it just wasn't fair.

Quite unprepared for Joe's tears, his mother stopped shouting and looked at her distraught son. Sitting down on the edge of the bed, she said, calming down, 'Who has taken them then if it's not you? Nobody else has been in the house. Joe, I'm sorry for shouting at you, but I just don't understand where they're all going. Come here. Let me give you a hug.'

And they both sat on the bed, still puzzled and a little worried about the missing socks. Joe cuddled his mother and secretly wondered what was happening.

Joe wasn't the only one to be wearing odd socks. At school that day, lots of his friends were complaining about the problem too. Though there were funny moments like when one of the male teachers was obviously wearing flesh-coloured tights and looked very uncomfortable, especially since it was his turn to give an assembly. There was a lot of sniggering and nudging as the new teacher, Mr Armelsnoup, talked about looking after those less-fortunate, and it didn't help when he asked volunteers to come out and help with his assembly.

As each pupil walked to the front of the hall, they peered down at his shoes with the tights showing.

That night, when he arrived home, Joe found his mother going through all the drawers upstairs and lining up rows of socks – all old and faded; they had seen better days. 'Mum, what are you doing?' he asked, staring at the rows.

'Well, you're going to have to wear all these old and small socks until the others turn up. I don't know what you do with them, Joe,' his mother stated crossly as she sorted out the socks.

'I think we have a phantom sock snatcher who sneaks in when we're all asleep…' began Joe, making up the first thing that came to his mind, even though it sounded far-fetched.

Trying to be good, Joe went to his bedroom to start his homework, still wondering where all the socks had gone. He also thought about the conversations he had had with his friends in earlier days about the same thing. What was happening to all the socks? Then he laughed to himself at the thought of Scotland Yard police force holding a sock investigation, or the prime minister holding a sock conference, or having questions in the Houses of Parliament about the developing sock crisis.

He wondered whether the members of the army, navy, air force, marines, police and secret service were also wearing different-coloured odd socks.

Joe decided to set a trap to see if there really was a phantom sock snatcher. After saying goodnight to his parents, with his mother scolding him about the socks – again, Joe went to bed. Well, that's what his mother and father thought...

Back in his bedroom, Joe placed a basket under the window and the lid of the laundry bin by its side (to catch the thieves). He put a reel of nylon rope from the garage by his bed and left a drawer open to tempt his sock snatcher. Fastening the cord of his dressing gown tight, he snuggled underneath the bedclothes, his nose and eyes peeping out, ready to catch this phantom sock snatcher.

Chapter 9

As it grew dark, Joe tried not to feel tired. He thought about his football and rugby matches and how he was going to play in them. Outside the sky was dark, but the stars were sparkling and so bright, almost like lights in his house. He couldn't fall asleep.

Joe waited and waited for something strange to happen.

Nothing happened.

He counted sheep, cars, football players,

new trainers and baseball caps – anything to keep awake. He found it difficult to keep from nodding off and then woke abruptly, angry that he'd allowed himself to miss a moment.

He heard his mother having a bath and getting ready for bed, and then his father checking the doors and lights and turning on the television in their bedroom.

Still nothing happened.

He heard the light and the television go off.

Everything was silent.

Joe waited, still snuggled underneath his bedclothes, his eyes darting everywhere, scouring the shadows for hints of the thieves. Now sure there was no such thing as a sock snatcher, he reluctantly began to drift off to sleep, trying to keep his eyes awake but failing to do so. Every now and

then he would wake up, sit upright in bed, look around his bedroom and then fall back into his slumber.

It was the scratching on the windowpane which woke Joe. It was the tiniest grating sound. Pulling down the duvet and gripping it tightly, he stared at the window and waited to hear the scratching again. Outside the midnight sky sparkled with stars illuminated like fragments of diamonds.

Joe saw something peer through the window. He could see three tiny faces with pointed ears, scaly skin and bulging eyes scanning the bedroom. The creatures turned to each other, ogled at the room and huddled, deep in conversation.

Joe couldn't believe what he was seeing.

He rubbed his eyes.
He sat up in bed.
He clutched his bedclothes.

And he waited. He watched as the creatures came through the walls as if by magic.

Joe wiped his eyes again. He stared again. The three creatures chatted to each other and looked quickly around the room. Their small green frames, dressed in yellow tunics with pointed boots, moved slowly around the bedroom and then went quiet. Joe, now gathering his wits, was just about to scream. Suddenly, a larger, much larger, creature came through the wall, nodded to the others, turned to Joe and said very gently, 'Hello, Joe. We thought you'd be awake one night.'

The creature had large brown eyes and slightly-rounded ears. He wore a brightly coloured coat and, on his head, a long, trailing cap.

'We love your socks…' said Beezo as he stared at the surroundings in the bedroom.

'They've come in very handy for the garden and they're growing so well…' added Breanok from behind the Wumple Chumple, lugging a large, glittering bag and perching on the bed. He fell flat on his back and gave a loud yawn and snuggled into the duvet. Joe watched, speechless.

'And we're growing some of your socks into trees…' added Bendrick very proudly, standing as high as he could and then crossing his small, knobbly legs as he also sat on the bed. 'You're not going to scream, are you?' questioned a yawning Beezo. 'It would be such a shame, since we're really very nice – aren't we?' He motioned, waving his knobbly hands to the others, who nodded in agreement and smiled.

The three little Idgits nodded at Joe, then at each other, scrambling and bouncing up and down on the duvet. They giggled and gabbled to each other, oblivious of Joe.

Suddenly, Beezo said, 'We've got loads of beautiful sock trees. You should see them. I love the purple and orange ones the best…' He chuckled, twiddling the duvet with his fingers. Joe couldn't quite believe what he was seeing and hearing.

The Wumple Chumple stood by the window in view of the magic cart and ponies, holding a golden sack. He listened to the Idgits and watched Joe's reaction to their questions and comments. He smiled at Joe as if to reassure him that the events were harmless and that he would be safe. He watched as another Idgit spoke to Joe about the socks back in his own world.

'Mine's the garden. You should see all the rows of beautifully coloured socks looking wonderful in the blue grass. You'd love them…' gabbled Bendrick to Joe.

Chapter 10

'STOP!' whispered Joe, trying to confidently take control of the most bizarre experience. He did not want to wake his parents, who might find this all frightening. Unable to think of anything else to say, he got out of bed and

towered over the creatures with his hands on his hips, and demanded

silence. This was his bedroom. The

Idgits looked at Joe with his arms folded as he firmly asked them to be quiet. Shocked, the mischievous creatures stood motionless, quiet as mice. The Wumple Chumple looked on as Joe told the Idgits off. Then, turning to him, Joe asked, 'Just exactly who are you? Where do you come from? AND why are you here?'

They all stared at him after at his outburst, then the strange, short creatures smiled at each other and laughed. In fact, they rolled and roared with laughter, their round, extended stomachs shaking up and down as they gurgled and blue tears rolling down their faces.

'You'll wake my parents! Stop it now.'

One by one each of the Idgits stopped laughing and quietened down until they were just gently sniggering. The Wumple Chumple listened to Joe, sympathising with his problem and frustration with the Idgits.

Then Breanok suddenly babbled to Joe about his world, why they were here in his bedroom and about the magic globe. 'Joe, we really like it down here. You should come and play with us someday in our world and see all our beautiful sock trees. We were looking in the magic globe with the Wumple Crumple when we saw something terrible. We're all off to save these two children who have lost their parents in a catastrophe. We're going to save them, Joe. Come over here and look into the globe and see them. Come on, over here.'

The Idgits beckoned Joe over to the globe, which was shining and glowing in the dark room. Joe hadn't noticed it before. The Wumple Chumple beckoned for Joe to join them. 'Just look at their pain, Joe. How can anything be so bad?' the Wumple Chumple asked, fixing his eyes on the picture of the children crawling in smoke and crying for their parents.

'I told you lot, we shouldn't have ever found that magic globe,' grumbled Beezo, tugging at his comrades with the Wumple Chumple clinging to the sphere.

'MAGIC GLOBE?' echoed Joe.

'Oh yes,' replied Breanok. 'The Wumple Chumple was happy until he found it hidden under a mound back home. Out there somewhere,' he added, pointing to heavens outside.

Beezo and Bendrick found three odd pairs of socks from his drawer, which were far too small to wear now and put them into the sack. 'Love these ones, Joe. We collect socks to make things with, to grow sock plants and trees. They make everything look so bright. We've been doing it for ever, and use socks for the tiles on our roofs. We even thought about cooking them, but decided the colours would be spoilt. By the way, Joe, can you eat socks or use them to flavour food?' queried Bendrick, waving some patterned socks in the air to show the other two Idgits, who nodded.

Joe didn't answer. He didn't know what to say. Once again he was speechless. Stuffing the socks into the bag, the Idgits returned to the globe and waved Joe over. Gingerly, he tiptoed and leant over the swirling sphere. Hidden deep in the curves of the globe were the faces of two heartbroken children, wailing for their parents. They looked ravaged and torn, their eyes clouded with terror, tears cascading as they clung to each other amidst the falling debris of buildings. Joe couldn't quite work out where the children were, but the landmarks did look familiar.

Then, studying the globe and pointing at it, he suddenly exclaimed, 'I know where this horror is taking place! It was on the news the other day! I can't remember where it is exactly – but it's thousands of miles from here.'

The Idgits and the Wumple Chumple stared vacantly at each other, then at Joe.

'Well, we have to go and rescue the children,' replied the Wumple Chumple, gathering up some of the old odd socks to blow his nose. 'I will plant these and grow some more socks,' he muttered.

'You really are the Phantom Sock Snatcher, aren't you?' quizzed Joe.

Just as he finished the sentence, he heard his mother bounding towards his bedroom, shouting at being woken up by the talking and noise from Joe's bedroom.

'What's the matter with you, Joe? Can't you sleep? And who on earth are you talking to?'

With that, she flung his bedroom door open to find the Idgits checking the socks once again in the glittering bag, the Wumple Chumple covering the magic globe and Joe standing nearby. 'AAAAAAAAHHHHHHHHHHHH!' screamed his mother, looking at the strange creatures.

Chapter 11

Trying to act as if the scene in his bedroom was normal, Joe cleared his throat and looked at his mother. It was too late to hide the Wumple Chumple and the Idgits in his bedroom, so Joe knew he'd have to deal with his mother's reaction.

Standing next to the creatures and waving his hands at them, he said, 'Mum, can I introduce you to the Idgits and the Wumple Chumple. I know this looks far-fetched and like something out of a film. They're not from our world. They're from outer space and are on a mission to save two children.'

He nodded at the Idgits, who smiled and bowed their heads.

Joe's mother stood still, her mouth open in disbelief at the sight before her eyes. Not in a million years could she have imagined seeing this spectacle in her son's bedroom.

'Hello, Mrs Joe's Mother!' chimed the Idgits in unison, nodding to her and smiling.

The Wumple Chumple waved at her, wafting one of Joe's dirty football socks in front of her face.

She sat numb.

Unable to speak.

Unable to move.

Unable to comprehend the situation.

Putting her hands into the pockets of her blue dressing gown, she stared at Joe, who appeared quite relaxed at the unreal and strange situation.

Joe could tell she couldn't work out whether this was a dream, a joke or some weird party. He thought she would feel helpless, as Joe knew his mother always liked to be in control of events. So, trying to ease her panic, he moved to be near her.

At this moment the Wumple Chumple announced his intention to save the children. 'Well, we have to continue on our journey now,' he said. 'It's getting late and we have a lot of flying to do.'

Joe looked on helplessly. Helping the children sounded so wonderful, and he secretly wished they would ask him to go with them on this adventure.

The Idgits spun around and said in unison, 'So Joe, and Mrs Joe's Mother, will you come with us tonight? We might need you. I know this is a lot to ask. But you might be able to help us.'

This wasn't how the evening was supposed to develop. Joe was meant to go to sleep, nothing more. She watched the creatures huddle together and whisper and Joe's mother felt even more uneasy.

They smiled at her then continued their conversation. After a while, the creatures turned and stared at her. 'We will need you to tell us about these people from the globe and guide us. We might get lost, and we will need you to direct us to the place where all this is happening,' said the Wumple Chumple gently. Joe and his mother nodded. Everything was very confusing. She was sure she was in the middle of a dream, or was it a nightmare?

'Mrs Joe's Mother, we have a magic blanket to keep you warm. We'll take you to the children. And, Joe, you can come too,' commented Breanok.

'Come on, we need to go... I don't think we'll have time to get more socks from

Joe's friends, or anywhere else. We need to go,' added Beezo.

So, putting the globe into the sack, they disappeared through the wall. The Wumple Chumple followed suit. Joe and his mother sat on the edge of the bed, bewildered at the encounter with these charming creatures from another world.

Coming to his senses, as if he was waking from a trance, Joe shuffled to his bookcase and, turning to his mother, asked, 'Shall I bring my atlas of the world so we don't get lost?' Nodding blankly not really listening, she watched as he stuffed a small pocket atlas into a pyjama pocket, along with a pencil and pad.

Chapter 12

Joe and his mother stared in confusion at the wall. When they wanted to get anywhere they opened doors – they didn't go through walls. They had never walked through a wall before and didn't think it would work.

Suddenly, a hand emerged through the bedroom wall, beckoning, and a voice shouted for Joe's mother to hold on. Without thinking, she did. And, before Joe's eyes, his mother disappeared through his bedroom wall. He peered out and saw her sitting in the cart, the magic blanket wrapped around her. Waiting for the hand to come through the wall again, Joe grabbed a jumper and wrapped it around his waist. Then he put on some thick boots and remained still.

Finally, a knobbly hand pushed its way through the wall and beckoned to Joe. With one hand clasping tightly on the atlas, pencil and paper, he entwined his other hand with the creature's. His heart thumped like a gong, so loudly he could hear it as well as feel it. As the green hand clasped his, Joe's body edged towards the wall, which suddenly felt like jelly. His arm was the first thing to slip into the wall. This was followed by his shoulder, then one leg, and then suddenly his whole body slithered through the bricks. Joe didn't feel anything as it happened, but it all looked dark and it seemed ages before he appeared at the other side.

Joe and his mother sat in the magic cart, unsure of what to expect. After being handed a blanket, they both waited for something to happen.

The blue ponies reared into the air as the Wumple Chumple whispered to them. The Idgits held on to the rims of their seat and waited for the ponies to build up speed. The Wumple Chumple pulled the reins taut, the ponies reached up their legs, ready to stride into the sky, and the magic cart tipped back slightly. Suddenly, they shot into the evening sky like an exploding cannon or rocket.

They rode through the midnight sky, the Wumple Chumple sitting at the front of the golden cart and the Idgits singing at the top of their voices. The wind blew softly, the stars twinkled and shimmered as they galloped past, while the blue ponies chatted to each other, laughing as stardust sprinkled and sprayed them like showers of joy.

Huddled under the magic blanket, Joe

'HHoLDDDD oONN!'

felt as warm as toast. The heat was just perfect. He was still unsure about this experience, but he knew that he was part of something magical. He also knew this may never happen again. He decided to enjoy this adventure.

He saw his mother sitting next to the Wumple Chumple in the cart. Wrapped in her magic blanket, she was staring intently at the Wumple Chumple and Idgits.

They could see the globe of the earth swirling in the atmosphere, and while it was difficult to recognise countries, the oceans were easier to point out. Gliding in and out of the galaxy, they skimmed the rays of the stars.

Mesmerised by the events, Joe didn't

notice the cart stop in the midnight sky. The ponies halted, motionless, whilst the Wumple Chumple and Idgits poured over the magic globe and his mother stared into the skies and galaxies, smiling contentedly as if it was a beautiful dream.

The Wumple Chumple began crying again. The Idgits, not noticing their friend's plight, were deep in conversation with each other, whilst every so often a pony cocked its ear to listen to the stars zooming through the sky.

Puzzled as to why they had stopped, Joe peered cautiously over the edge of the cart, down at the world below. Joe wondered when they'd start moving again.

Impatiently, the ponies turned their

heads and softly muttered something to the Idgits, then waited. After an intense discussion between the Wumple Chumple and Idgits, the reins shook. The ponies once more reared up and leapt

into the midnight sky.

They galloped with all their might, anxious to make up time. As the speed increased, the cart swayed back and forth – a bit like the waltzes at the fair – and the speed of the air pierced Joe's face and hands. They whistled past the stars, which now looked like clouds and plumes of faded gold melting into the dense black skies.

Breanok suddenly yelled out, 'Hold on, Joe and Mrs Joe's Mother! We're on our way down now and it may get a bit tricky! Mrs Joe's Mother, sit with young Joe. Sit still – this is going to be a steep landing. You must...'

With that, they dived through the sky. Joe and his mother clung to each other with fear and excitement. The cart thumped and thudded through the clouds.

It twisted and spun around. Staring out, Joe saw the ponies in control. The Wumple Chumple guided them gently to a specific place, whilst the Idgits gave directions from the globe to their leader. The Wumple Chumple listened intently to their instructions.

Chapter 13

The cart shuddered to a halt. Joe and his mother crouched under the blankets and waited. They could hear yells, screams, whimpers and people scurrying. The

tranquillity and beauty of the journey through the sky with the Wumple Chumple, the Idgits and the blue ponies had changed. They had landed at their destination, a place now dominated by anger, aggression, terrible pain and chaos.

Peeping out from beneath the protection of his magic blanket, Joe saw buildings lying shattered and a black, heavy smoke smothering cars and the remnants of houses, and clinging like glue to those shuffling and wandering, aimlessly seeking help. Something terrible had happened. Many of the people were cut, bruised, badly injured, limping and crying for those lost.

Stretching out, straining as far as he could, Joe noticed fires in the mountains. He eyed shattered buildings and trees which lay like mounds on the ground, covered by a blanket of choking smoke, while people cried. Immediately surrounding the cart were groups of people shouting at the strange-looking guests who had 'popped' out from the sky on blue ponies.

This was a far cry from the happy and contented place the Idgits and Wumple Chumple had left before landing at Joe's house. Now the atmosphere appeared dangerous, and so many people needed help.

Although confused, some of the wailing and hurt children smiled or stroked the ponies just for a moment and then carried on. Nobody laughed at the Wumple Chumple or Idgits, as the devastation of their own surroundings consumed their thoughts.

They heard a cackle of conversations in a language neither Joe nor his mother understood, as the people questioned each other. Realising the strangers weren't going to hurt them, Joe stood up in the cart, wrapped in his golden blanket. The onlookers stared at him, bowed their heads and muttered to each other.

Joe didn't know what to expect and, like his mother, waited for some instructions.

'I know what's happened…' said Joe in a flat, numb voice as he shook his head. 'I know what's happened. There's been a disaster, maybe a tremor or earthquake activity. I don't know how we can help those children when everyone needs help,' continued Joe.

His mother squinted. Everything here looked confusing and very sad. The Wumple Chumple stared at the terrible sight and turned to the Idgits to ask something. Joe and his mother concentrated as the Wumple Chumple tried chanting a spell, but nothing happened.

'Can we send them all magic blankets to keep them safe? Or perhaps we could magic this all away!' the Wumple Chumple exclaimed, waving his hands and pointing at the scene before his eyes.

The Idgits examined him closely, hoping the magic would work.

Alongside his dazed mother and

speaking firmly, Joe turned and said, 'Wumple, in our world we don't have magic or sock trees or plant socks or blue ponies.'

'This is a different world,' added Joe's mother, eying the hordes of injured and shocked people. 'It sounds a great idea, but it won't work here. You can't just magic things away with socks and colour.'

Joe glanced at his mother as she spoke. He couldn't imagine any magic taking place – what it would look like, and what would happen. However, he didn't want to upset the Wumple Chumple and said,

'I think it would be wonderful if you could use your magic spell book to make everything better' he blurted out remembering how the Idgits and the Wumple Chumple had travelled and then slid through the wall.

'I want to help these people, so I'll use my trusted spell book. We'll see what we can do to stop this anguish,' replied the Wumple Chumple.

He felt tired, unhappy and unsure. The Wumple Chumple hadn't seen a disaster before. Nor had he seen so many people crying, or so many crumpled buildings. His plan to save the children in his globe now seemed small and pointless as so many people needed assistance. He wanted to save everyone, and hoped his magic would work. He hadn't cast a spell from his book for a long time.

'Now we're here, what are we going to do?' asked Joe, keen to start helping.

Suddenly, the Idgits disappeared into the crowds. The Wumple Chumple, Joe and his mother got out of the cart, debating what course of action they should take.

'We must help them,' whispered the Wumple Chumple, wiping tears from his eyes. 'They would love my sock trees and plants back home.'

Joe watched as people looked at him, but they didn't scream or cry out at the colour of his skin; everyone was too worried about finding their families.

'Mrs Joe's Mother, what can we do to make things better?' the Wumple Chumple asked gently.

'Wumple, I really don't know. It looks like something terrible has happened, perhaps an eruption. I don't know. Probably thousands of people need help, not just one or two children. This devastation will go on for miles if it's an earthquake. Thousands of people will need aid and support. How can you help them?'

Joe's mother looked thoughtful as she wiped tears from her eyes. The agony of the people was unimaginable.

Joe scrutinised his mother and wondered if she was coping with all the surprises of the night. Nothing surprised Joe any more.

Chapter 14

The Wumple Chumple, delved into the sides of the golden cart and brought out a black, battered, leather-bound book held together by a spiral coil. As it opened and the pages turned, Joe was convinced he heard them speak, making a gurgling, snurgling, spluttering and bluttering sort of noise.

Joe had never seen a book talk. He

watched as it responded to its reader, like two friends trying to solve a problem. He noted every movement intently as the Wumple Chumple and the spell book worked together to find a successful charm.

Joe and his mother both stared at the Wumple Chumple frantically flicking through the spell book covered by a misty golden shadow. He was nodding and waving his arms in the air, stamping his feet and snapping his fingers. At one stage the spell book bellowed as it hissed and spat plumes of grey smoke. It was becoming exhausted trying to find the right spell.

In desperation the Wumple Chumple tried making up new spells, angering the book in the process. But each one failed miserably. So the book bawled, and the Wumple Chumple yelled at himself.

Every so often he'd fling the book to the ground, the pages crying, howling and shouting as they scattered everywhere. Then, in a panic and flurry, apologetically, the Wumple Chumple scrambled to gather the pages before they wafted away and placed them firmly back in the book. Then there was a contented purr and a sigh: the spell book was happy.

Suddenly, the Wumple Chumple spun around, his eyes sparkling and shining like piercing diamonds. Delighted, he shouted to Joe and his mother, beckoning them to him.

'There! I think I might have found some

magic to help. Listen to me…' he began.

His voice sounded strange, deep, hollow and quivery, startling both Joe and his mother a little. They clung together, not sure what to expect. The ponies swished their manes and tails in air and waited for the magic to work.

'I can help! We can help! LOOK!'

At that, the Wumple Chumple pulled back his head and shouted to the sky.

Joe's mouth opened wide.

His mother's eyes opened wide.

The people were speechless too.

The Wumple Chumple screamed,

stamping his feet and performing some sort of dance. It wasn't what Joe had expected, but it did look magical – and a little alarming. The spell book jumped out of the Wumple Chumple's hands and darted through the air, making a sharp screeching noise. It

weaved through the air, diving in and out of wrecked buildings and remnants of greenery, while the Wumple Chumple continued his chanting and rhythmic movement. Nothing happened.

The ritual continued, the Wumple Chumple putting even more energy into the spell, whilst the book's swirling and twirling became frantically fast.

Still nothing happened.

Joe began to think their attempts were all in vain. Then, as the Wumple Chumple tried to work his magic along with the spell book, the heavy dust and grey clouds gradually began to evaporate into the sky. At first it was tops of trees and any high buildings which looked clear. The smog was lifting. Bit by bit, it thinned out into a hazy film which covered everything near to the ground. Then the last remains disappeared into the sky like a plume of smoke.

Still immersed in their pain, people didn't notice the air. They continued to cough and gasp for clean air, amidst their crying. However, they became more aware that they could notice everything around. Now that the dust and smog had vanished, survivors were able to see the extent of the damage for themselves. And this wasn't easy, as men, women and children scrambled to dig out the rubble from the buildings to find lost family members.

From the cart Joe could see the enormity of what appeared to be an earthquake. Not only had the air become clearer, the spell seemed to have improved the injuries of the people who were now able to move more easily.

He wasn't sure this was what the magic was supposed to do, but he was delighted. The Wumple Chumple watched intently as those around him move more ably, and he was pleased with the results of his hard work. Mesmerised, Joe watched as men, women and children walked with a little more ease. Their scars and injuries disappeared and they looked stronger.

Chapter 15

There was a sense of hope. The blackness was evaporating and the air seemed easier to breathe. The land still looked the same, but the fires had died down and people were now helping each other to find relatives and friends.

Although pleased that the spell had made the injured much stronger, the Wumple Chumple was still sad.

'I can't change what has happened to your world. I did try, but the spells didn't work, even with the help of my spell book,' croaked the Wumple Chumple, his voice sore from shouting his last spell. 'Some things we can't change, but some we can, eh, ponies?' he added as he patted them tenderly.

'Using your special powers to help these people was a wonderful act,' stated Joe's mother.

However, her kind and supportive words couldn't mend the heartbreak of the Wumple Chumple.

Realising how important these events were across the world, Joe knew there would be television crews around, wanting to get interviews with anyone who had assisted. He didn't think it would be easy for the Idgits and the Wumple Chumple to understand the media, and they might be confused by the attention. Joe felt very protective towards them.

He turned and said, 'Wumple, there will be people who want to interview you and thank you for casting a spell with the incredible use of the magic book. And it is amazing how you tried so hard to stop the pain and suffering. Everyone will ask you about the blue ponies and the magic cart. Are you ready for this?'

The Wumple Chumple looked blankly at Joe. He didn't understand.

As he stood by the ponies, patting them, people began coming up to thank the Wumple Chumple for saving them. A man, still limping but smiling, came up to the Wumple Chumple along with his family. Choking with emotion, he said, 'I don't know what you did, or what magic you used, and I don't care what you look like. I just want to thank you for doing something that has helped us all.' With tears in his eyes, the man and his family shook the Wumple Chumple's hand, Joe's hand, Mrs Joe's Mother's hand.

Slowly, the crowds began to realise that magic had helped them, and many more came to thank the Wumple Chumple and the strange visitors who had landed in a cart from the sky.

Then Joe's prediction proved correct. Journalists that had been monitoring the disaster crowded around the Wumple Chumple like a migration of vultures. Joe heard the click of cameras and saw the flashes of the lights.

Suddenly, someone stuck a microphone into the Wumple Chumple's face, ready to ask questions. Then another person rushed with a brush to wipe his coat clean, whilst another tried to wipe his face and add some makeup! Joe watched in rage as reporters ignored the plight of the survivors and concentrated on getting an interview with the strangers from space.

The Wumple Chumple remained quiet. He stood, still stroking the blue ponies, amidst the frenzy surrounding him. 'Where are you from?' asked a reporter, nudging through the throng. The Wumple

Chumple looked dazed but not panicked. 'Why and how did you cast your magic?' shouted another reporter from the back. 'Why do you have odd-coloured skin and why are your ponies blue?' questioned another anxious reporter.

At once an avalanche of questions exploded and the Wumple Chumple bowed his head. Joe ran to his side and cuddled him. The reporters went quiet and still, shocked to see this new hero crying.

Jumping out from behind the crowd and making her way to the front near the ponies, Joe's mother shouted,

'This is the Wumple Chumple and he has tried to save your people from this horror. I don't know where he comes from, but Joe and I have flown through the sky with him. He told us that he was here to save a little boy and girl. He saw them in his magic globe! He has tried to support you all, though he didn't need to. So give him some space, and stop crowding round him. Can't you all see he may not be used to this sort of attention?'

Chapter 16

By the time Joe's mother had finished venting her fury, the crowd was silent. It was at this point she realised that she was wearing her dressing gown, and she wondered if it was the right colour for the cameras. If she'd known that her evening was going to be magical and very dramatic, especially in front of cameras, she would have worn her best dressing gown. And

maybe she'd have gone to the hairdresser's to have a trim or blow dry! Furthermore, she would have made Joe wear his best pyjamas too!

The quietness and stillness was broken by the gabbling of the Idgits, who were talking about finding new socks. Joe couldn't believe that amidst all this mess the Idgits were concerned with gathering socks. How odd and selfish, he thought as he witnessed the looks of misery on the faces near him.

'Look what we've found!' squawked Beezo, waving some socks in the air.

'We've found millions of them for planting! They're all different colours...' added Beezo. 'We won't have to borrow Joe's anymore! We've got a massive sack of them.'

With that, the Idgits bounced onto the cart.

'And, Wumple, you'll never guess what… we found the two children in the globe hiding in forest. We got lost, so we walked and walked, coming across lots of injured people in a terrible state. We stayed a while, taking in what was happening. Then we forgot about time and just kept wandering amongst the buildings, people and huge mounds of earth.

We walked, and the further away we went, the fewer people we saw. Then we came upon a small shelter with a rusty roof. Peering out from a window were some people.

As we drew nearer, we recognised the faces, and once we were close, we identified the children from the magic globe.'

'Then, Beezo, what did you do?' asked the Wumple Chumple, who had been listening closely.

'We told them that you were going to help them – try to save them. So now we know where the two children are and you can cast a spell,' added Breanok.

'We could let them stay with us until they are well,' added Bendrick. 'Come to think of it, should we take all the children and look after them and let them stay with us? They can always come back when things are more settled here,' he said, unaware that the silent crowd was watching his every movement and the cameras were filming him for news coverage.

After considering the Idgit's idea,

Joe's mother spoke. 'That's a wonderful thought, but I don't think it will work. All the children will want their parents and family,' she replied. She could see the television crews filming their conversation.

Joe added, 'Yes, I'm sure they would be much happier with their parents. If I had the choice, I know I would be.' The Idgits looked at each other, then gazed at the crowd surrounding the ponies, Wumple Chumple, Joe and his mother.

'What shall we do, Wumple?' asked Bendrick, turning to him as he stroked the ponies. 'After all, we did come to save the children.'

'We could just take the socks…' chirped Beezo.

'They have wonderful colours here…' added Bendrick.

The Wumple Chumple wondered what to do.

Fascinated and not wishing to lose this wonderful moment, the reporters stayed still and quiet and just watched keenly every action of these strange beings.

'What else can we do? I must do something!' responded the Wumple Chumple.

'I think you should just do another spell – or some magic – and keep everyone with their families. I think you should cast your spell on everyone,' Joe said.

Walking towards the growing crowd, the Wumple Chumple nodded in agreement at

Joe's wise words. Once again he began his strange ritual to create the magic needed to help all those wounded or looking for family. Joe's idea was the best solution and one which would result in happiness. The crowds and the cameras were silent.

They waited whilst the Wumple Chumple and spell book prepared for more magic.

'Oh Wumple, I'm not sure I can do this anymore! I think I may let you down and fail these lovely people. I'm finding it so hard to get the spells right!' spluttered and groaned the spell book.

Looking on sympathetically, the Wumple Chumple patted the cover of the book and replied, 'This is fine, dear friend.

I am sure we can do it. Come on, this can be our last spell – and what a wonderful one it will be! Come on. Just try once more for the children, the people and this world! I know you can cast a spell!' The book gave a gentle bleat and its pages ruffled as the Wumple Chumple tapped it.

Everybody stood still. The crowds looked on in awe. The television crews went quiet. The newscasters stood motionless.

Viewers across the world, in every country, stopped in their tracks.

The Wumple Chumple was changing colour, dancing, vaulting into the sky, yelling the strangest words at the top of his voice, next there came a loud whirling – almost, a wailing, a wheezing. The spell book danced and twirled through the air, flapping its pages and bellowing some strange and deep noises. At one stage the book appeared to expand and fill the sky, and the spells and potions popped off its pages and onto the crowds below, evaporating into mist as they touched the heads or ground.

Then, without warning, the spell book grabbed the Wumple Chumple and dragged him into the air, hurled him through plumes of black, smothering smoke, bawling as it cast a spell. The Wumple Chumple knew this was his last chance to save the people. Clenching the book with all his strength, he bounded into the skies jumping from cloud to cloud, chanting a spell with his book, which changed size and colour as it moved. Both were a sight to behold as they roared and roared, filling atmosphere with chants and different spells until the onlookers felt dizzy with the noise.

Suddenly, a thick, smoky black cloud settled on the people, buildings and landscape, hiding any fragments of light. It looked bleak, cold, almost worse than the devastation.

Moments later, the noise died down. Joe couldn't see the slightest outline and he felt frightened. He could only hear the quiet chanting of the Wumple Chumple finishing his magic.

The thick, gooey cloud lifted. The sky

was bright, the sun shone, the flowers were waving in the gentle breeze... and everything looked perfect.

Slowly, life returned to normal. People were no longer limping, or crying for family. Buildings, trees, bridges and monuments now stood proud, whilst in the distance Joe could see roads jammed with traffic and hear horns hooting loudly.

Joe scanned the view to spot the girl and boy from the magic globe. He couldn't find them amongst the throngs of people rushing from place to place.

Although delighted at the new picture of happiness, Joe found it strange that there were no traces of the earthquake. He knew the Wumple Chumple's magic had worked and he had made the transition appear so easy and normal. Then Joe remembered, that was what magic was meant to do! He watched the transformation before his eyes in awe. Nobody was ill, injured or maimed, and the buildings and vehicles were fine. There were no craters, no toppled buildings and no crushed vehicles. He still tried to see if he could spot the children, but it was pointless as the place was so busy.

Chapter 17

Everything appeared normal. Joe gazed at his mother, and at the three Idgits.

People were going about their daily business as if nothing had ever happened. Joe knew the magic had been successful, but he couldn't work out if the people could remember anything. He looked, puzzled, at his mother, who just smiled.

'I think I know what's happened. The Wumple Chumple has taken them back in time to before the earthquake, and he's cast a spell to prevent it from taking place.'

At that, the Wumple Chumple came to the cart, tired from the effort of casting the spell, sat down with the spell book.

Wiping his brow, he beckoned them near to explain what he had done.

'Well, Joe and Mrs Joe's Mother, I think we finally got it right. Everything is back in its place as before. Nobody will remember a thing about the earthquake. And the children are back with their parents, so they are safe,' said the Wumple Chumple to them.

The Idgits listened and smiled. The adventure had been very successful.

'Now, we must prepare to go home. We have finished saving these people and can leave them now, and the children in the globe will be fine with their parents' the Wumple Chumple added.

Joe stared at his mother, then at the

people, buildings and the Idgits, who were now getting the ponies ready to fly. Joe felt sad. He had enjoyed the exploit with the Wumple Chumple and the Idgits. He didn't want it to end.

He felt tired – his eyes were heavy, and he began to yawn. The Wumple Chumple guided Joe to the cart and carefully wrapped a magic blanket around him and tucked him in. Then, clutching a huge

sack of multi-coloured socks, the Wumple Chumple stood over him as he drifted off to sleep.

Feeling relaxed and in a slumber, Joe could only hear snippets of conversation between the Wumple Chumple and his mother. They were talking about visiting the Wumple Chumple's land, far away from Earth.

He didn't see the stars smile and nod as the ponies sped through the sky at the speed of light. Nor did he see the cart and its occupants head towards his house and hover outside the bedroom window.

He didn't feel the Idgits carefully place him back in his bed, all warm and wrapped up. He didn't see his mother hug the Wumple Chumple, the Idgits and the beautiful blue ponies and pat the old spell book.

'Well done, dear old friend of Wumple's. You did a great thing, to help save these people. You are the best spell book ever!' she said tenderly as she touched the book, which was now firmly closed.

It opened, and a weak, tired voice responded, 'Well, dear Mrs Joe's Mother, what an adventure – and at my time in life, as an old, doddery spell book. I enjoyed it very much, and am delighted to have helped so many people. But I now need to sleep!' And with that it closed and began snoring.

Joe's mother was now sad at saying

goodbye and she began to cry as the Wumple Chumple lifted her into the bedroom as well. She said, drying her eyes, 'Please come back again. We'll leave lots of socks for you to plant. Please come back. We loved our adventure with our new friends.' Beaming between her tears, she waved to her new friends and glanced at Joe, who lay asleep, smiling in his dreams.

'Mrs Joe's Mother, you have been wonderful and we will come back again,' replied the Wumple Chumple, sad at leaving his new friends, but knowing it was necessary. 'But we have a present for all your hard work. Look up to the sky.'

Joe's mother raised her head and saw a formation of large, twinkling stars closely joined together in the shape of a sock. She gasped with delight.

'Tomorrow morning, a new constellation will be announced and it will be called… Joe's Sock. This is our present to you. You won't remember anything, but someday we will return to help others with our magic globe.' The Wumple Chumple gently kissed Joe's mother, and then he shot off into the night with the Idgits and disappeared into space.

Chapter 18

Joe was jolted awake by the alarm going off and screeching in his ears. Nudging it with his elbow to stop it ringing, he felt his mother's dressing gown. Slowly, he opened his eyes and asked why she was there.

'I don't know why I'm lying on your bed, Joe. I must have come into your room to get your uniform ready for school, then fallen asleep here,' said Joe's mother, looking in

confusion at the golden blanket on top of the bed. 'I had a strange dream that I was flying through the sky with you and we went to a place where there'd been a disaster. I can't remember much more, but it felt real, as if I was there. And I don't know why we have this golden blanket. Do you know anything about it, Joe?'

He shook his head. He then added, 'It's weird. I had a dream last night with you in it – and some creatures from a different world. I dreamt we travelled in a golden cart and there were some blue ponies and small creatures with green skin…' His voice trailed off as he remembered tiny bits of the adventure, but he couldn't piece them together. Everything was a blur.

Joe's mother replied, 'Well, maybe it was something you watched on TV which made you dream. Anyway, you have to hurry up and get ready for school.'

She straightened her dressing gown and left to make breakfast.

Joe could hear his father downstairs getting very excited about something and he wondered what it could be.

'Joe! Quick! Joe, now! Come and see this! It's amazing!'

Charging down the stairs, Joe sped into the kitchen to see why his father was excited. He couldn't believe his eyes. Scientists had reported that a new constellation of stars in the shape of a sock had appeared in the sky overnight. Nobody knew where the stars had come from. There was a frenzy of activity across the globe and reporters from all over the world were interviewing astronomers in America, Russia and China to try to explain this incredible sight.

And even more amazing- it was going to be called Joe's Sock!

The stars were headline news, the main story. The second story was that, for unknown reasons, a predicted earthquake had failed to happen after week of tremors.

Again scientists were trying to understand how this had happened. Of course everyone was delighted the disaster hadn't taken place

'Our second big story is that an earthquake has been avoided. A team of experts are confused as to how and why this has happened – it remains a mystery. All we know is that scientists had been measuring rumbling in an area of northern China for a number of weeks and predicted a powerful earthquake any time soon. But this morning the earthquake movement had completely disappeared,' said the newscaster, unable to hide her amazement at the main stories. Joe looked at his father. 'I'm sure I know something about those main stories, or was it part of a dream?'

'I'm sure that we'll find out,' said his father. 'Fancy having a new constellation of stars and fancy having them named after you!' His mother added,

'By the way, Joe, have you got any socks for school today? Did you find the new ones I bought for you?'

His mother grinned as Joe shrugged his shoulders and munched his toast.

Meanwhile, the Wumple Chumple was planting rows of socks, making sure they didn't clash. He sighed. How wonderful his life was and how happy he was with the results of his new adventure. Smiling at the socks, he wondered when he would be visiting Joe and Mrs Joe's Mother again.

Checking the growth on his sock plants, he gathered any spare ones, bungled them into his bag and made his way up the hill to his little home with the brightly coloured tiles. Everything was perfect with the world.

Puzzles

Spot the 6 differences
Image one

Spot the 6 differences
Image two

Design your own sock patterns & colour them!

Join the dots

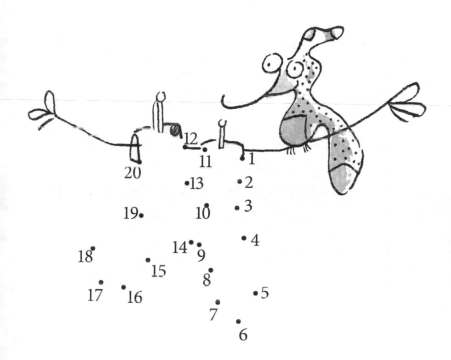

Word Search

Find these words in the word-search below.
(Forwards, backwards, upwards, downwards, and sidewards, but NOT diagonal)

Beezo   Phantom
Bendrick   Ponies
Breanok   Snatcher
Globe   Sock
Idgits   Wumple

A	D	W	B	C	B	S	X	W	H	T	E
U	D	U	I	K	O	N	A	E	R	B	S
E	I	M	A	J	X	L	R	O	A	U	T
N	H	P	O	N	I	E	S	R	B	Z	I
M	X	L	P	S	J	W	B	E	A	C	G
O	O	E	B	E	I	J	E	H	F	E	D
T	T	Z	K	G	V	G	N	C	M	W	I
N	X	P	E	W	C	L	D	T	U	G	Y
A	Y	B	K	E	H	O	R	A	J	M	P
H	Q	O	G	S	B	B	I	N	S	R	A
P	L	H	T	Y	V	E	C	S	S	C	Y
S	K	C	O	S	U	U	K	V	B	G	H